The World's Greatest Treasure

by Rita Jaglowski

Illustrated and Revised
by Dorene Terryberry

East Derry, New Hampshire

This story is dedicated to
my beloved sister Margaret
who has always been
a lighthouse in my life.
Thank you for giving
my children their first Bible.

The World's Greatest Treasure

A precious Bible, fresh and new

Went home to live with Emma Lou

"This book", she thought, is for the birds"
And did not read the living words

But that was long ago...now look

Is this poor thing that very book!

The cover now so loose and worn

Revealing pages lost and torn

An added note and scribbled word

Erased the place she never heard

The Noah's Ark, entirely gone-

With long lost cords of a David song

Now tossed aside for the rummage sale

along with the tale of the Jonah whale

Among all the rummage now readied for sale

The Bible so Holy seemed common and frail

Beneath, behind, and treated like junk

The treasure of God was hid in a trunk

Yes, hid in a trunk instead of a heart-

God's love without measure He longs to impart

The morning arrived for the sale to begin

Precisely at nine, bargain hunters rushed in

The items were grabbed and flung without care

So nobody noticed it fly through the air

The hall of the church, all chaos and noise

As one looked for clothes, another found toys

The Holy Book trampled,

Was kicked open wide

Exposing hid treasure,

It harbored inside

No words can describe the old lady's pleasure,

To hold in her hand, the world's greatest treasure

THE GOSPEL
ACCORDING TO
SAINT JOHN

She gently replaced it's leather bound cover

And that's when her heart skipped a beat to discover

The name of her niece,

Engraved there in gold

On a throw away thing

To be bartered or sold

She'd given it once

To her own Emma Lou

Instructions from God,

Meant to see, hear, and do

The memory of caring now brought forth a tear

She hadn't seen Emma for many a year

So right then and there, Aunt Ruth was to pray

That Emma find Jesus that very same day

"May Emma, my niece, renounce every sin,

And open her heart for the Lord to come in"

Aunt Ruth lived in Jesus, His Word lived in her

Whatever she asked Him was sure to occur

A clock somewhere chimed at half past the nine

All things work together in God's perfect time

With no place to go,

Emma stood at the door

At the end of herself looking

Pale, thin and poor

Missing pages of promise,

Were clutched in her pocket,

Old Noah's bright rainbow,

And Aunt Ruthie's locket

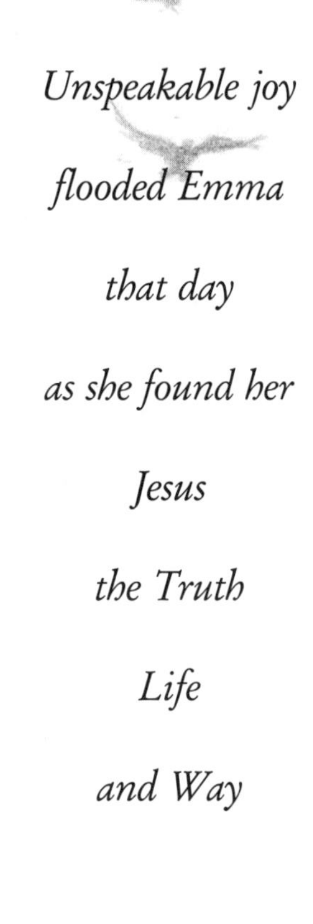

Unspeakable joy

flooded Emma

that day

as she found her

Jesus

the Truth

Life

and Way

The angels drew near to hear her sweet voice

"Thank you, Lord" she exalted, and heaven rejoiced

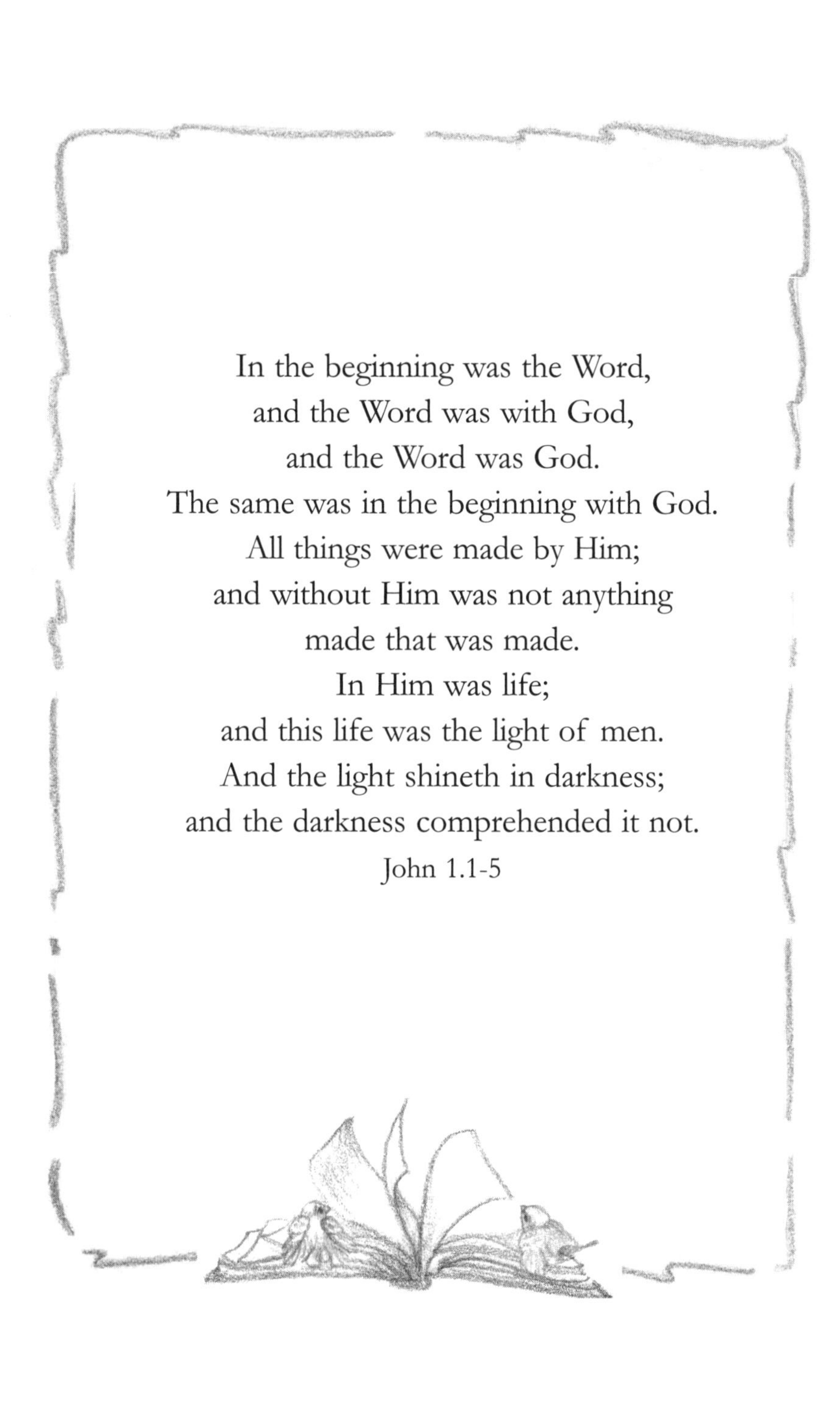

In the beginning was the Word,
and the Word was with God,
and the Word was God.
The same was in the beginning with God.
All things were made by Him;
and without Him was not anything
made that was made.
In Him was life;
and this life was the light of men.
And the light shineth in darkness;
and the darkness comprehended it not.

John 1.1-5

Prayer to accept the free Gift of Salvation

Heavenly Father, I believe that Jesus was born of a virgin, died on the cross and on the third day God raised Him from the dead for the forgiveness of sin.

Jesus come into my heart and forgive me of all my sins and cleanse me from all unrighteousness. I repent for all my sins. I surrender all of my life to You. I confess that Jesus Christ is my Lord and Savior.

Amen

For whosoever shall call upon the name of the Lord shall be saved.

Romans 10.13

For with the heart man believeth unto righteousness: and with the mouth confession is made unto salvation.

Romans 10.10

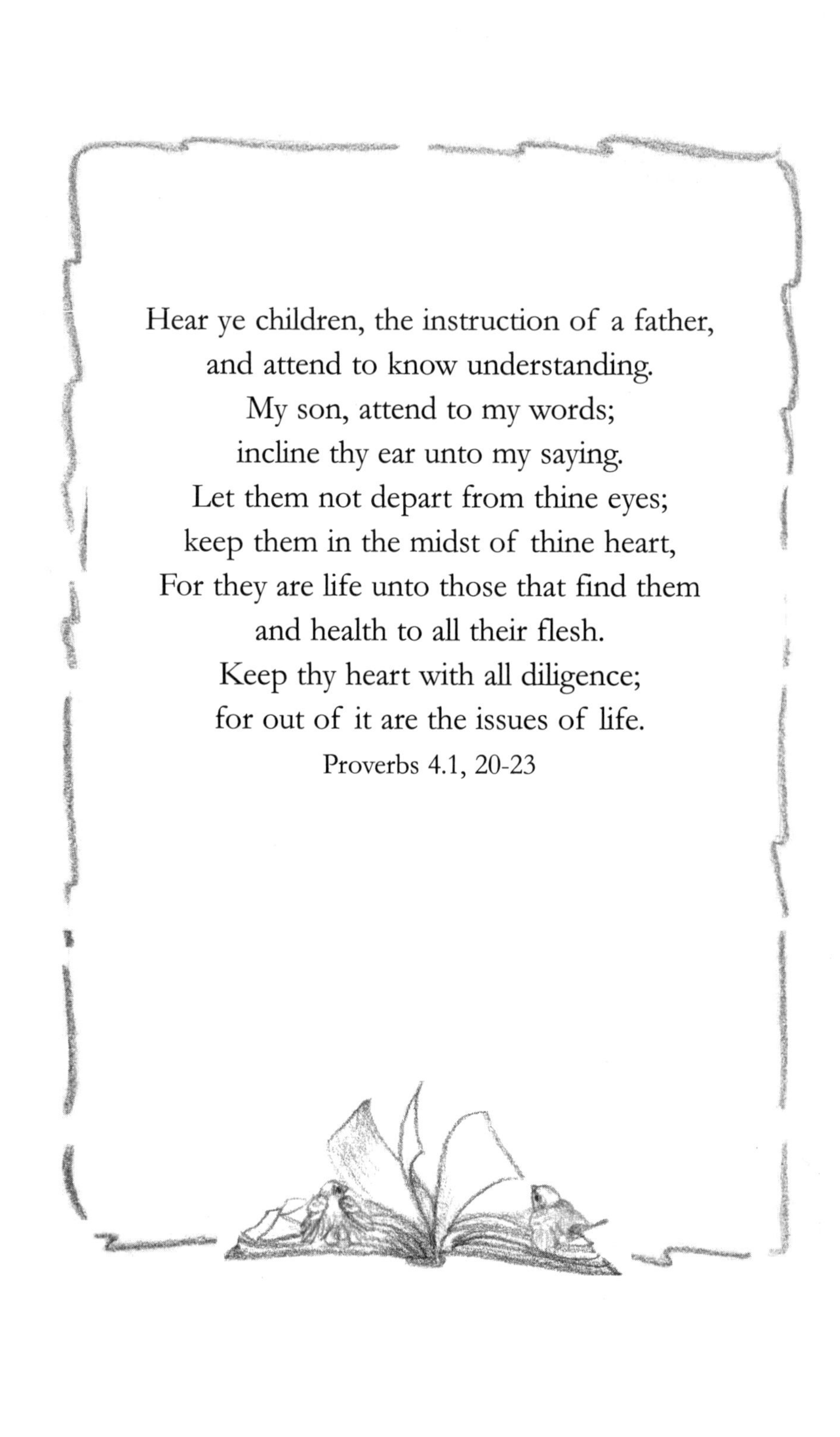

Hear ye children, the instruction of a father,
and attend to know understanding.
My son, attend to my words;
incline thy ear unto my saying.
Let them not depart from thine eyes;
keep them in the midst of thine heart,
For they are life unto those that find them
and health to all their flesh.
Keep thy heart with all diligence;
for out of it are the issues of life.

Proverbs 4.1, 20-23

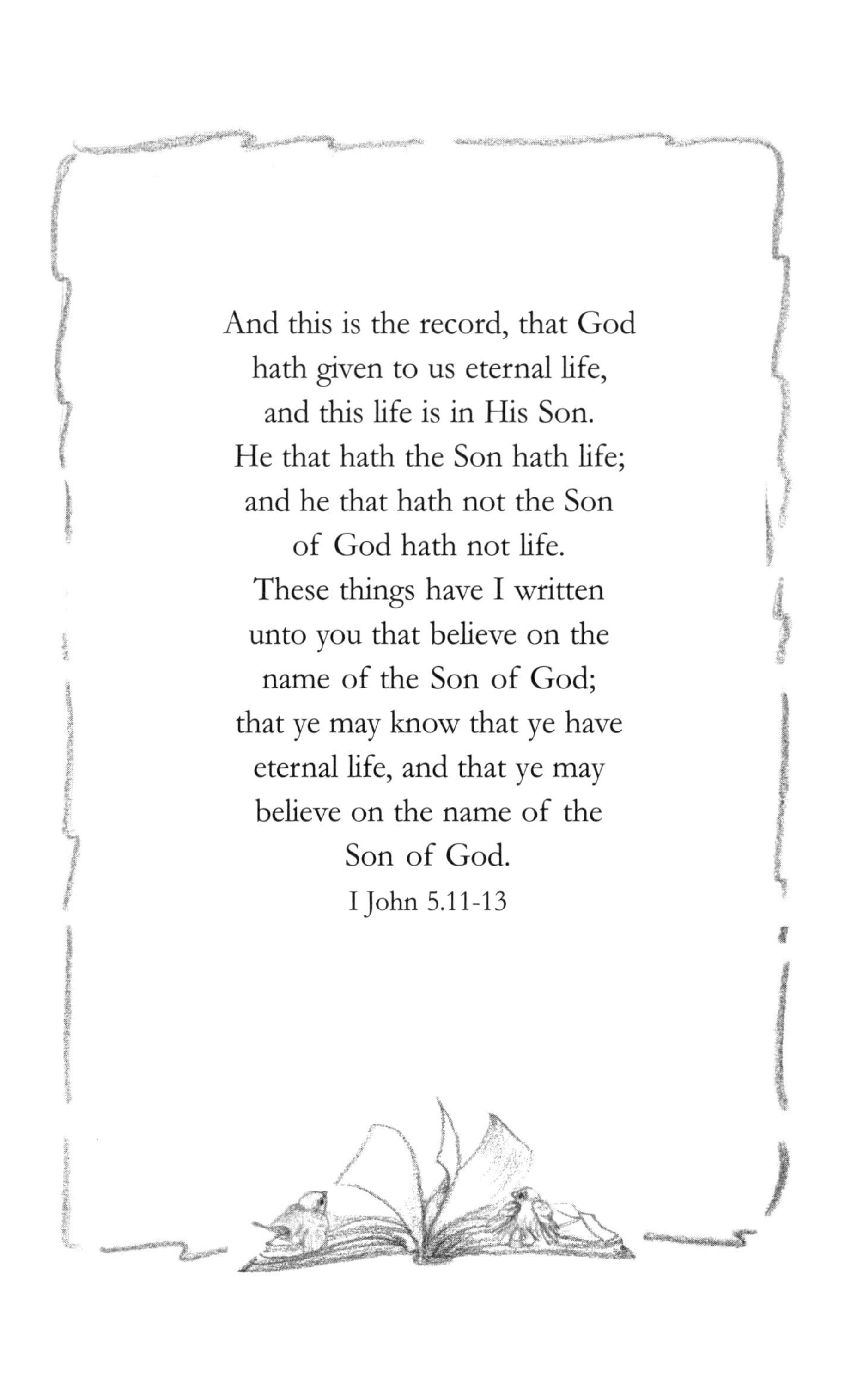

And this is the record, that God
hath given to us eternal life,
and this life is in His Son.
He that hath the Son hath life;
and he that hath not the Son
of God hath not life.
These things have I written
unto you that believe on the
name of the Son of God;
that ye may know that ye have
eternal life, and that ye may
believe on the name of the
Son of God.

I John 5.11-13

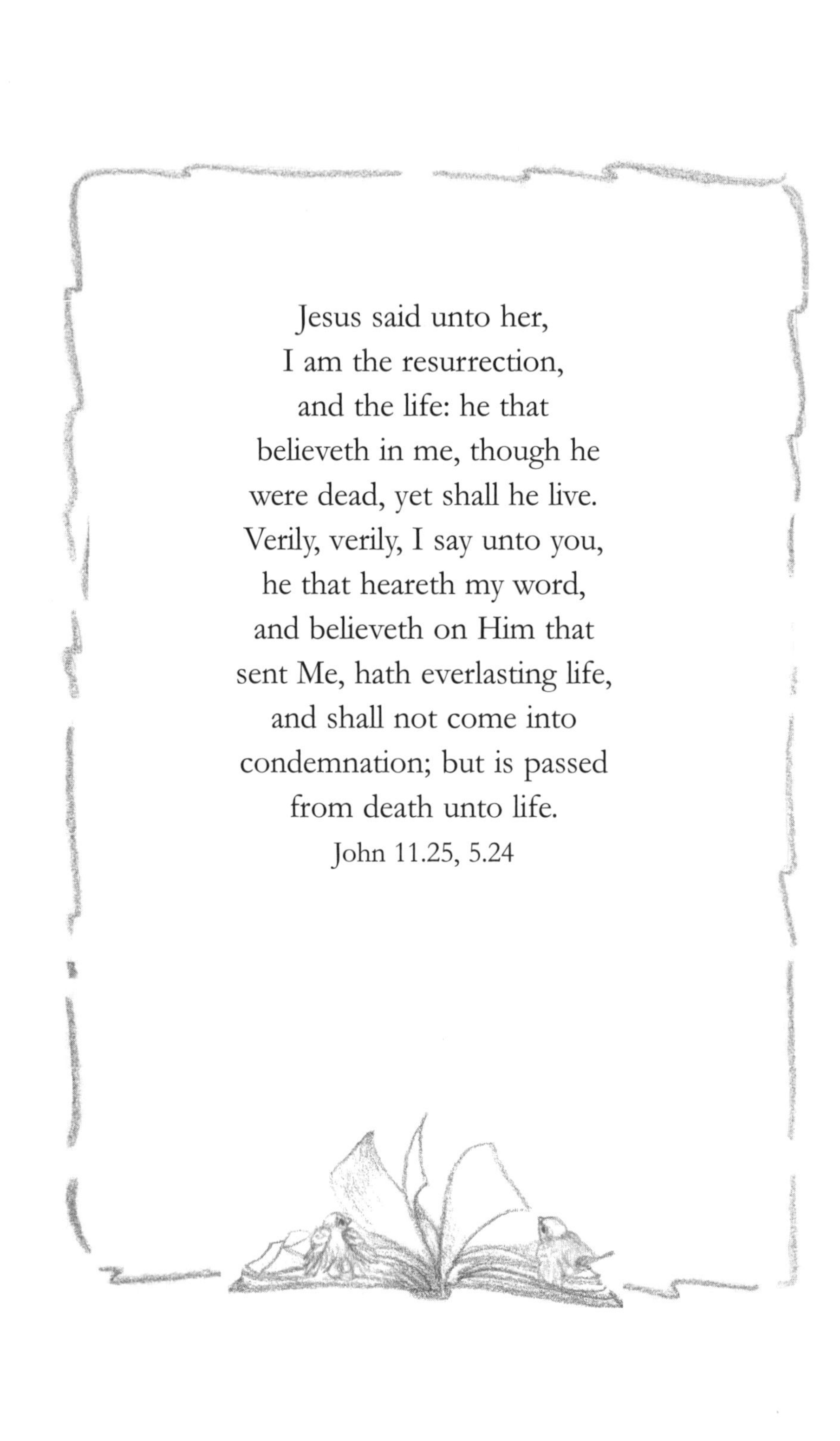

Jesus said unto her,
I am the resurrection,
and the life: he that
believeth in me, though he
were dead, yet shall he live.
Verily, verily, I say unto you,
he that heareth my word,
and believeth on Him that
sent Me, hath everlasting life,
and shall not come into
condemnation; but is passed
from death unto life.

John 11.25, 5.24

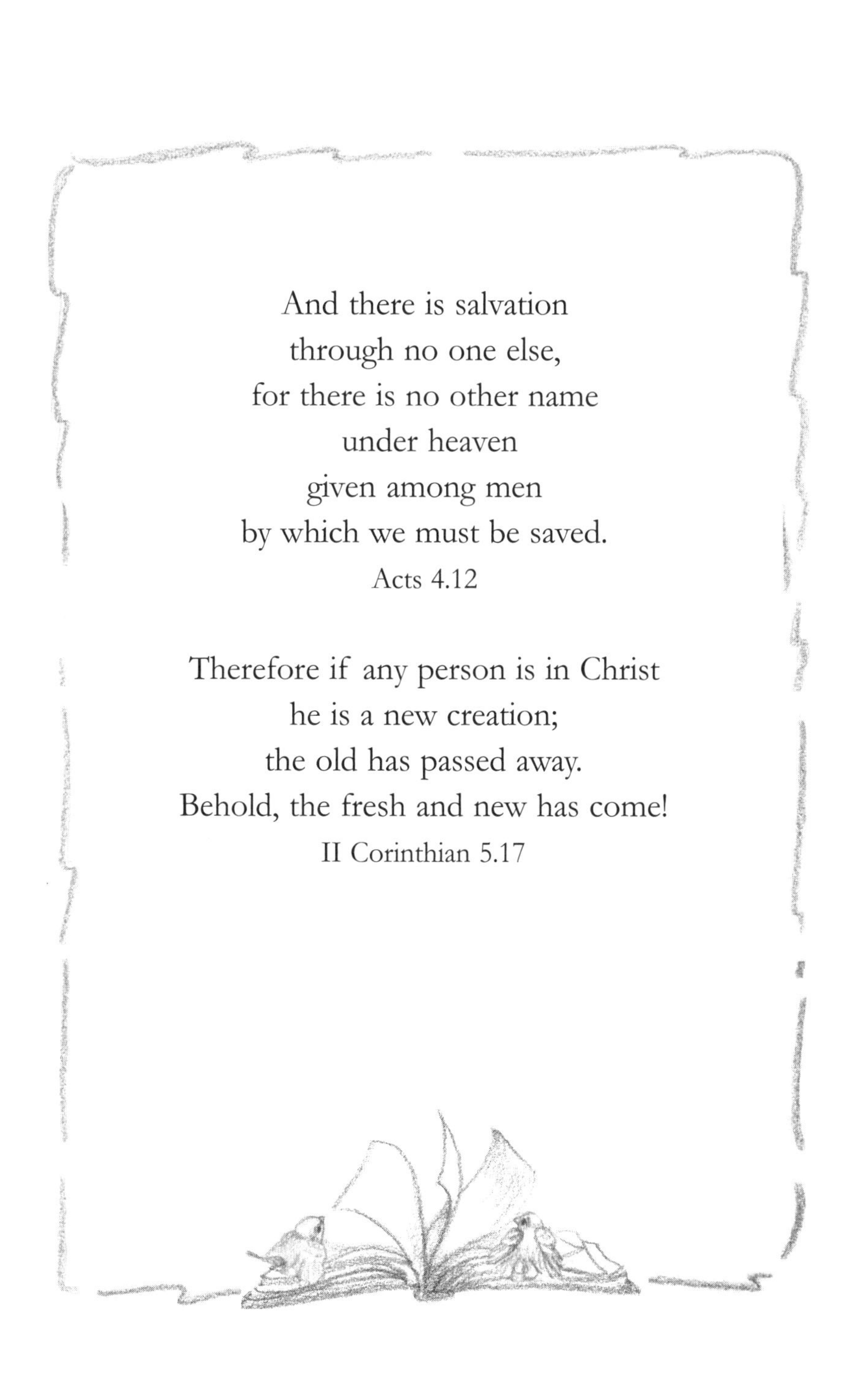

And there is salvation
through no one else,
for there is no other name
under heaven
given among men
by which we must be saved.
Acts 4.12

Therefore if any person is in Christ
he is a new creation;
the old has passed away.
Behold, the fresh and new has come!
II Corinthian 5.17

P.O Box 86
East Derry, NH 03041
603.432.WORD
SownbytheWind@msn.com